The Spirit of the Wild West

by L. L. Owens

Perfection Learning® CA

Illustrations: Rex Schneider

About the Author

L. L. Owens grew up in the Midwest. She was given her first diary on her sixth birthday. And she's been writing ever since.

She studied English and journalism at the University of Iowa. She has worked as a reporter, a proofreader, and an editor. And her interests include literature, film, music, and cooking.

She loves to read about almost anything. And she has always been fond of biographies—especially about interesting American women. So she had lots of fun learning and writing about Annie Oakley.

Ms. Owens now lives near Seattle with her husband, Timothy Johnson.

Image Credits: Art Today pp. 7 top and middle, 23 top, 26 top, 29 top, 30 top and middle, 31 top and middle, 34 top and middle, 35 top and middle, 38; Art Today from *Campbell's Illustrated History of the World's Columbian Exposition*, pp. 5, 6 bottom, 7 bottom, 8, 10, 11, 12 bottom, 13 bottom, 14, 15, 18 bottom, 19, 24, 25 bottom, 26 bottom, 27, 28 bottom, 29 bottom, 30 bottom, 31 bottom, 32, 33 bottom, 34 bottom, 35 bottom, 36 bottom, 37 bottom, 39 bottom, 40 bottom, 41 bottom; Denver Public Library, Western History Department pp. 18, 25, 28, 39, 43, 44, 53, 54; Library of Congress pp. 6 top, 12–13 top, 20, 22, 23 bottom, 40 top, 48; Western History Collections, University of Oklahoma Library pp. 21, 51

Perfection Learning® Corporation, 1000 North Second Avenue, P.O. Box 500, Logan, Iowa 51546-0500.
Phone: 1-800-831-4190 • Fax: 1-800-543-2745
perfectionlearning.com
Paperback ISBN 0-7891-2854-3
Cover Craft® ISBN 0-7807-7850-2
Printed in the U.S.A.
5 6 7 8 9 10 PP 10 09 08 07 06 05

Table of Contents

CHAPTER 1

A Day at the Fair

Emma Claire Smith plopped down on a marble bench. She sighed. She took a big gulp of fresh lemonade. She'd had a long morning at the fair.

"There, now," said Mama. She stroked Emma's curly brown hair. "Doesn't that taste good?"

"Yes," Emma answered crossly. Then she quickly glanced up. She knew she shouldn't speak to Mama that way.

Mama ignored Emma's tone. At least this time she did.

She so wanted Emma to have a good time. After all, here they were at the Grand Exhibition of 1893—the Chicago World's Fair!

"Let's rest a few minutes," said Mama. "Then we'll go back to the Woman's Building. We can look at anything you want. You liked the paintings, didn't you?"

Mama continued. "In a little while, we'll meet up with Papa and your brothers. We can all have lunch together. How does that sound?"

Emma took her time answering. She and  Mama had argued about chores on the way to the fair. And Emma was still pouting.

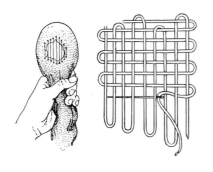

"I hate chores!" she'd announced. "I'd rather be outside with Papa and the boys."

"We've been over this, Emma," Mama had replied. "The boys help your father. I need your help around the house. I know you don't like it. But that's how it has to be."

"It's not fair," Emma whined. "They get to have all the fun. All I do is mend their socks. And do their wash."

"I suppose you'd like to plow the fields with them," Mama had said. "And bale the hay. We've all got our chores to do. Life is full of hard work. And you'll have even more to do when you're older."

The fight rang in Emma's ears. "Mama just doesn't understand," she thought.

"Emma? Did you hear me?" Mama asked sternly. She meant business. And Emma knew it.

"That sounds okay to me, Mama," Emma replied. She hadn't really heard what Mama had said. But she knew the right answer!

Inside the Woman's Building, a wall of bright fair posters caught Emma's eye. Emma eagerly looked them over.

"She's here!" Emma shouted. She'd found what she was looking for.

"Who is?" asked Mama.

Emma's big brown eyes flashed. "Oh, Mama, you know!"

Then she pointed to a big poster. It was for Buffalo Bill's Wild West show.

The poster showed a pretty black-haired woman. She wore a wide-brimmed hat, a fringed skirt, and a flowered deerskin jacket. With a wink and a smile, she aimed her rifle—straight at Emma!

Mama nodded as she read the poster.

CHAPTER 2

Emma Sneaks Away

It was noon. Mama and Emma headed toward the Midway.

Emma felt happier now. Mama had promised to take her to Annie Oakley's evening show. But that wasn't until 8:00. Emma didn't think she could wait that long!

Annie Oakley was her hero. Emma figured Annie never had to bake or do the wash. She had more fun things to do.

"Mama?" Emma asked as they walked.

"Yes?" Mama answered.

"Can we go to the show early? To meet Miss Oakley? She could make you see. I just know she doesn't have to do housework," Emma said.

Mama pressed a finger to Emma's lips. "Not another word, Emma Claire. Understand?"

Emma nodded. She pictured her life as Annie Oakley. There'd be no boring chores. That was for sure.

11

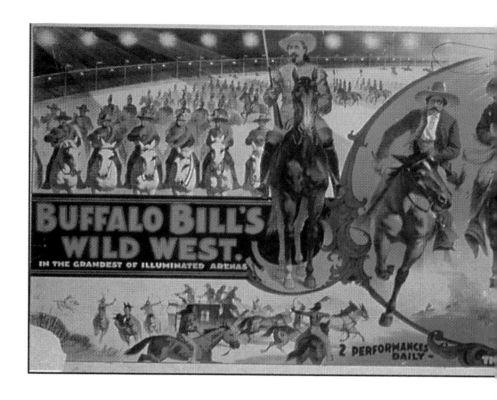

"There must be some way I can meet her," Emma thought.

Mama dug through her bag. She took out a map of the fair.

"Let's find our meeting place," Mama said brightly. "There it is. We need to go to G-7 on the map. We're at F-15 now. That's not so far."

Mama folded the map. She began to put it back in her bag.

"Wait," Emma said. She held out her hand. "Can I hold onto it for a while? I might want to look for something."

"Of course," Mama replied. "Just don't lose it."

They soon saw Papa and Seth, Emma's oldest brother. Both were waving their hats over the crowd.

"Where's Gabe?" Mama asked Papa.

Gabe was Emma's other brother. Gabe was 12. At ten, Emma was the "baby." Her brothers loved to tease her about that.

"He'll be along," answered Papa. "He's taking a look at the Ferris wheel."

Papa gave Emma a quick, one-armed hug. Then he added, "There's a place to eat right over there. I told Gabe to meet us there."

"He's on his way now," said Seth. "I can see him."

Seth was very tall. He was even taller than Papa. He'd turned 15 over the summer. And it seemed as if he'd grown three feet!

Gabe rushed to Papa's side. "I'm starving!" he announced.

And with that, the family made their way to the food building.

Everyone chatted excitedly through lunch.

"You should see the Ferris wheel," said Gabe. "They say it's 264 feet tall."

"I saw an amazing dishwasher!" Mama exclaimed. "It does your work for you!"

Seth told about the Electricity Building. "There's a really nifty gadget. It's called a kinetoscope. It shows pictures of real people. Moving pictures!"

Papa said, "Well, you wouldn't believe what Gabe and I saw. We went to the Animal Show. Lions were riding horses. And tigers were riding bicycles!"

"No!" said everyone at once. Everyone, that is, but Emma.

She was gone! She'd slipped away from the table. And nobody had even noticed.

CHAPTER 3

Little Sure Shot

Emma ran across the Midway. "I just *have* to meet Annie Oakley!" she thought.

Emma unfolded Mama's map. "Hmm," she said. "Looks like I follow the Midway a bit farther. Then I turn right on Madison. Left on 62nd. I cross the railroad tracks. And there it is. On 62nd and Hope."

Emma made it to the site in no time. A huge sign read—

BUFFALO BILL'S WILD WEST
America's Greatest Entertainment

She walked right onto the campground.

It was about three hours before the afternoon show. Cowboys were napping on the grass. Indians were playing cards. Band members were trading stories.

Emma stared. Then a voice from behind surprised her.

"Are you lost, little girl?"

Emma spun around. She came face to face with a young man. He was carrying a rifle!

18

"I'm not lost," Emma replied. "And I'm not little, either."

"Is that so?" His eyes twinkled. "I'm Johnny. I'm with the show. What can I do for you?"

"I need to speak to Annie Oakley," Emma stated.

Johnny chuckled. "Oh, you do!"

"It's very important." Emma stood her ground.

"I'm sorry," he said. "Miss Oakley is resting. She won't see any visitors now."

"But I need her help," pleaded Emma. "I want to be like her. Maybe even join the show someday."

Johnny took a step back. He studied Emma. Then he said, "You're a good shot, are you?"

Emma didn't reply. But she thought, "I'll let him think I can shoot. Maybe then he'll let me talk to Annie."

"Okay, Little Sure Shot!" hooted Johnny. "Let's see what you can do."

He pointed to a row of bottles in the distance. And he offered his rifle to Emma.

Emma tried not to panic. She'd only fired her father's gun once. And he'd held it the whole time. She knew one thing. She could never hit those bottles!

Just then, a small woman appeared.

"Johnny," she said sternly. "Did you just call this gal Little Sure Shot? Now you know that's *my* nickname!"

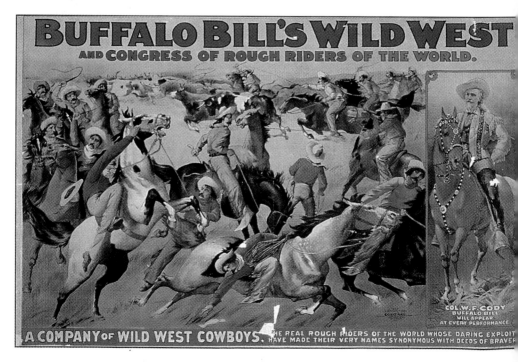

Emma's jaw dropped. It was Annie
Oakley! She was so pretty. She was much
prettier than in her pictures.

Johnny blushed. "Sorry, Miss Annie. I
was just playin' around. This girl here says
she can shoot. She wants to join the show."

"Is that true, young lady?" Annie stared
into Emma's eyes. And Emma froze.

CHAPTER 4

New Friends

All at once, words tumbled out of Emma's mouth. "I'm so happy to meet you, ma'am. I've read all about you in the newspapers. I think you're the best.

"I was thinking. Maybe I *could* help with the show." Emma continued. "I know all about it. I can already do some things. I can run fast. And I can ride. I could learn fancy tricks—"

"Slow down," said Annie. "One thing at a time."

Annie grinned. "This gal has spirit. Don't you think so, Johnny?"

"Sure do!" he replied.

But then Annie turned serious. "First things first. Where are your parents?"

Emma's mind raced. She had forgotten about her parents. They were probably looking for her. But she needed a little more time with Annie.

"You do have parents. Don't you?" Annie asked again.

Still, Emma didn't answer.

"Someone got shy," said Johnny. Then he pulled Annie aside.

"I just thought of something," he whispered. "Maybe she's an orphan. Some local orphan homes bring the kids to the fair."

Annie looked back at Emma. "It's possible," she said. "Let's get her name."

"We'll tell the guards about her," Annie continued. "They can find out if anyone's looking for her. And we'll keep her busy in the meantime."

Annie and Johnny faced Emma.

"What's your name again?" asked Annie.

Emma hung her head. She kicked at the dirt.

Annie looked at Johnny. He just shrugged.

"Come on now, honey," said Annie. "You must have a name."

"I don't want to say."

"Why not? You hidin' from someone?" Johnny teased.

"No. It's not that!" Emma had to think of something to say. Fast.

"I–I–I just hate my name. That's all."

"Let me guess," said Johnny. "Is it Martha?"

"No," Emma replied.

"Berniece?"

"No."

"Frances? Agatha? Maude?"

"No."

"Stanley?"

"No!" cried Emma. She started to giggle. "Stanley!" she repeated.

"Let her be, Johnny," said Annie gently.

Johnny chuckled. "You're right, Miss Annie," he agreed. "I'd best go take care of that matter we talked about."

"Let me know what you find out," said Annie.

"Will do."

Johnny disappeared through the gates. But Emma had no idea why. He was going to report her to the fair's police.

Annie stared hard at Emma. "Do you really hate your name?" she asked. "So much that you won't tell it to me?"

Emma knew that Annie was trying to help her. She also knew it was wrong to lie. But she swallowed hard. And she did it anyway—

"Yes, ma'am."

"Well, I know something about that. I used to hate my name too." Annie paused. "Do you want to hear my real one?"

"Annie's not your real name?" Emma was suddenly curious.

"Well, it is. And it isn't," Annie explained. "I was born Phoebe Ann Moses. I kinda kept the 'Ann' part. That was okay. But—oh! How I hated the name Phoebe! And the other kids teased me about Moses."

She went on. "I took Oakley from a town outside Cincinnati. Oakley's where I beat my husband Frank in a shootin' match."

"You don't say!" exclaimed Emma.

"As a matter of fact—I do say!" replied Annie.

With that, Annie turned on her heels. She walked toward her tent. At the entrance, she turned around.

"Are you coming?" she called.

Emma hurried to catch up. And inside they went.

CHAPTER 5

Annie's Place

"Make yourself at home," Annie said.

Annie led Emma to a rocking chair.

"Would you like some tea?" Annie asked cheerfully. "I'm going to make some for myself. I'm out of my famous jelly cakes. But here. Have some peanut brittle."

Annie held out a big, round tin. It was filled with the candy. Emma took a piece. "Thank you," she said.

29

Annie busied herself making tea.

Meanwhile, Emma looked around. A pair of bright curtains framed the tent's opening. And thick red carpet covered the wooden floor.

The tent was brimming with wonderful things. Emma saw fresh flowers, cozy couches, satin pillows, shiny medals, and lots of souvenirs.

Soon Annie served the tea. She sank down in a matching rocking chair.

Annie followed Emma's stare. It was fixed on her sewing.

It looked like a girl's dress. There was a set of finely embroidered linens too.

"I just finished those sheets," Annie said proudly. "I tried some new stitches."

Emma's eyes grew wider.

"Oh," Annie continued, pointing to the dress. "That's for a new girl. She needs it for a skit. So I whipped it up for her yesterday."

Annie noticed Emma's look. "Tell me, child. Do you like to sew?"

Emma shook her head. "No, ma'am," she answered. She was surprised to hear that Annie did.

"No?" asked Annie, slightly puzzled. "I do so much of it. Habit, I guess.

"My husband likes to tease," she added. "He tells people to check my hands. If they don't find a gun, he says they'll find a sewing needle!"

"But, Miss Oakley—" Emma began. She stopped herself.

31

"What is it? What's on your mind?"

"It's just that—well—why would you keep doing those things?"

"What things, child?"

"You know. All that sewing." Emma looked around her. "And cooking and cleaning. Especially when you don't have to? Since you can shoot and all."

"I don't understand," Annie said.

"You're a big star. Why do you keep doing women's work?"

Emma searched Annie's face for the answer.

Annie was shocked. She set down her tea. She looked into Emma's confused eyes. Then she slapped her knee.

Annie Oakley laughed—

"*Women's work!*"

CHAPTER 6

Wise Words

"There's no such thing, honey!" stated Annie. "I learned that long ago."

Emma looked puzzled.

"Don't you see?" Annie said. "There is no men's work. And there is no women's work. There's just work. And it all has to get done."

Annie poured some more tea. The two sat back in the rockers. Then Annie shared some of her life story.

"I've always done all kinds of work," Annie started. "I had no choice. My Pa got sick when I was young. He couldn't farm anymore. Or deliver the mail."

Annie sighed and went on. "There were seven of us kids. Ma had her hands full. So we all had to pitch in.

"I learned to trap and shoot," Annie explained. "I trapped birds and squirrels. And I shot game."

"I loved to be in the woods. It was so peaceful. That's where I learned to hit my mark," Annie added.

Annie's steel-blue eyes narrowed as she thought back.

"I worked at a hospital for a while too. I had a mean boss. But I loved the children there. I tried hard to help them.

"At home," Annie continued, "We kids washed the clothes. Ironed. Milked the cows. Picked berries. When we finished one thing, it was time to do it again. I couldn't wait to grow up and get away. I figured I wouldn't have to do all those awful chores anymore."

Annie paused to see if Emma was still listening.

35

Emma was on the edge of her seat.

Annie said, "I've learned a lot since then. No matter what the job is, someone hates to do it. Why, I've known lots of men who hate to shoot. But they have to. So they can put food on their family's table."

Annie went on, "You say you hate to sew. But sewing's not work to me. It's fun. I sew

 for me. And for people in the show. I don't have to. But I do it anyway. Right along with all the things I don't want to do. Like looking after my

money. And painting our house back in New
Jersey. Do you see what I'm getting at?"

Emma frowned slightly.

Annie struggled to find the right words.
Then her face lit up.

"The hard part is to always do what
needs doing. No matter what you think."

Annie continued. "The people of the
real Wild West did that. They did it
together. And that's what Buffalo
Bill's show is about—the amazing
spirit of the Wild West."

CHAPTER 7

It's Almost Showtime

There was still no word from Johnny. So Annie showed Emma her scrapbooks and her gun trunk.

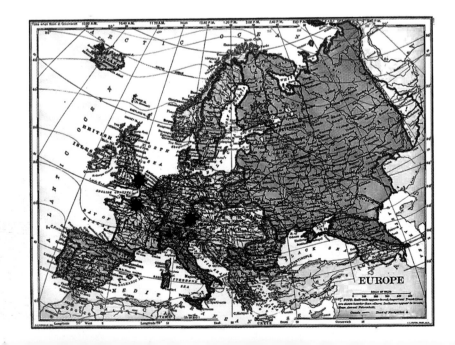

EUROPE

She told Emma about doing shows for
kings and queens. She talked about
traveling to London, Paris, and Munich.

Finally, it was time for Annie to get
ready for the show.

Buffalo Bill Cody stuck his head inside
the tent. "Half an hour to showtime,
Missie!" he said. "We're cutting out
the new ending. The little girl has
come down with a fever."

"Got it," said Annie. "Colonel—I'd like you to meet someone."

Emma had to pinch herself. It was really Buffalo Bill. And he was standing right in front of her! He was bigger than life. And his flowing hair gleamed in the afternoon sun.

"Charmed," he said, tipping his cowboy hat.

Then he looked as though he'd remembered something. He studied Emma's face. "How old are you, dear?" But before Emma could answer, Annie stepped between them.

"Colonel? May I talk to you?" Annie asked. "Outside?"

Annie was gone for a while. And Emma thought about her family.

"They're surely missing me by now. I should be getting back."

40

Then she thought about Annie's words. Emma realized something. Not finishing her chores had been selfish. She had run out to play last night. And she'd left behind a stack of mending.

Emma touched the new patch on her dress.

"What if Mama hadn't finished this for me?" Emma thought. "I know what. I wouldn't be wearing a clean dress right now."

Annie finally came back. She was alone. "I have a surprise for you," she said. She picked up the girl's costume. "Come here." Emma obeyed.

Annie held the dress up to Emma. She seemed pleased.

"Perfect! We'd like you to be in the show. Just for today. Think you can do the job?"

"Oh, I'll do anything!" Emma cried.

All thoughts of her family flew out of Emma's head.

CHAPTER

"Ladies and Gentlemen!"

Emma watched as the gates opened. Music blared. Fans streamed into the stands. Buffalo Bill's Wild West show had come alive.

The announcer roared—

"Ladies and Gentlemen! Presenting Buffalo Bill Cody! And his Rough Riders! They'll show you the real Wild West! The danger! The courage! The heartbreak! The triumph!"

Buffalo Bill bolted through the arena on his white horse. The crowd cheered.

The rest of the show was thrilling.

Annie galloped around the track. She shot on horseback, on foot, and on a bicycle. She shot from both shoulders and behind her back.

For her big finish, six glass balls were thrown into the air. Annie jumped off her

BUFFALO BILL'S WILD WEST.
CONGRESS, ROUGH RIDERS OF THE WORLD.

MISS ANNIE OAKLEY,
THE PEERLESS LADY WING-SHOT.

horse. She turned a handspring. Then she seized a rifle and hit the balls. Then she hopped back on her pony and rode away.

The audience went wild.

Annie ran back into the arena. She blew kisses to the fans. And she gave her trademark jump-kick as she left the stage.

Emma watched in wonder. She could see how skilled the performers were. She could also see that they took many risks.

43

Next came a thundering drumbeat. Indians did a corn dance. And cowboys rode bucking broncos.

Annie interrupted Emma's thoughts.

"It's time for your skit," she said.

Emma had forgotten! Fear gripped her.

"Oh, Annie!" she exclaimed. "Everything moves so fast out there. I can't do it!"

"You have to," Annie replied. "You promised."

"But I don't think I can!"

"You'd be surprised at what you can do. Now go take your place. Hurry up!"

Emma did as she was told. "Annie's counting on me," she thought.

CHAPTER 9

Spirit of the Wild West

It was time. A performer helped Emma into a stagecoach. It moved across a fake prairie.

Indians leapt from behind cardboard hills. One of them grabbed Emma right out of the stagecoach!

Emma was supposed to scream. And scream she did! She was caught up in the action. And at that moment, it seemed real.

Emma shrieked. The Indian placed her on his horse. And she let out a long, wailing cry.

The crowd was in an uproar. "Save the girl!" they chanted.

Arrows flew through the air. Rifle fire echoed in the stands. Buffalo Bill and his cowboys charged across the prairie. At a make-believe cliff, Buffalo Bill grabbed Emma. And he sent the Indian over the edge.

Emma forgot to stop screaming.

The crowd thought it was a joke. So they laughed. And they clapped.

Someone called out, "What's her name?"

The announcer turned to Annie. "Quick!" he begged. "What is her name?"

Annie smiled. She was proud. Emma had done her job. Even though she hadn't wanted to.

Annie whispered in the announcer's ear. Then he boomed—

"Let's give a grand welcome to the newest member of our show. A girl named Spirit! That's Spirit of the Wild West!"

The crowd cheered.

Buffalo Bill swung Emma onto his shoulders. They were still on his horse. And they took a lap around the arena.

Emma had calmed down. But she was still scared. There were so many people looking at her. It was loud. And the lights were hot and bright.

Just then, Emma saw two faces she knew.

"Mama! Papa!" she cried.

Buffalo Bill lifted her from his shoulders. Before her feet could hit the ground, she was in Papa's arms.

CHAPTER 10

Time to Go Home

Mama talked to Emma firmly.

"We have been so worried! We searched high and low. Luckily, these folks reported you to the police.

"And another thing," Mama went on. "You lied to these nice people. You told them you were an *orphan*. Really, Emma!"

"But, Mama," Emma said. "I never *said* I was an orphan. They just thought so."

Papa interrupted. "So you think that makes it all right?"

"No, sir," Emma replied. She hung her head.

Mama looked hurt.

Emma tried to explain. "I never meant to lie to anyone. And I didn't plan to be gone long. I just thought if I could meet Miss Oakley, maybe—"

"Maybe what?" asked Mama. "Maybe you could run away for good?"

"No, Mama. Really. I just wanted to meet her. I thought I wanted to be her. I figured she had an easy life. But she doesn't. She works hard. And she made me see why I should too. Why everyone should."

Mama raised an eyebrow. "She made you see all that? I guess I owe her a big thank-you!"

"No need, ma'am," chuckled Annie. She had a way of sneaking up on people. "It was my pleasure."

"Annie!" exclaimed Emma. "I did it!"

"You sure did, honey," Annie smiled. "I'm mighty proud of you." Then she looked at Mama and Papa. "You've got a special young lady here."

"Thanks for looking after her," Papa said.

"Here," said Annie. "I thought you'd be needing this." She handed Mama Emma's old dress.

"I'd like Emma to keep the costume. As a souvenir. From her one and only performance as Spirit of the Wild West!"

"We can't thank you enough," said Mama.

Papa gently pushed Emma forward. "Say good-bye to Miss Oakley. It's time to go."

"I'll never forget this day!" Emma stated excitedly. "Or you, Miss Oakley."

Annie kissed Emma's forehead. "I'll never forget you either."

Emma and her parents walked through the wide gates.

"We'd best go collect your brothers," Mama said. "They're waiting for us."

"Mama?" Emma said carefully.

"Yes."

"Thank you for mending my dress. I know that was my job."

"You're welcome," Mama said. She patted Emma's head. And she and Papa looked at each other.

"Don't you worry, though," Mama continued. "Papa and I have thought of plenty of exciting jobs for you. Seth and Gabe have too."

Emma looked up at Mama.

Mama didn't smile. But she winked.

"Oh, Mama!" giggled Emma.

EPILOGUE
The Real Annie Oakley

Phoebe Ann "Annie" Moses was born in Darke County, Ohio. Her birth date was August 13, 1860.

Annie's father died when she was nine. She helped feed her large family by shooting game. She became an expert shot.

Annie was raised to believe in herself. Her mother taught her that women were very important. This was a rare view in the 1800s!

Annie overcame shyness to become a performer. And her shooting career took off. Word of her talent spread throughout the area.

One day, she entered a shooting contest against Frank Butler. The match was in Oakley, Ohio. She won! She later married Frank. And took the name Annie Oakley.

Annie and Frank formed their own act. They joined Buffalo Bill's Wild West show in 1885. For 17 years, Annie was a main attraction.

The show was a great success. Annie made friends. And she had fans all over the world.

Annie and Frank enjoyed their time off too. They spent it at their beloved home in Nutley, New Jersey.

In later years, Annie continued to work. She followed a strict schedule. She practiced, exercised, and ate well. She helped poor children. She starred in several plays. And she gave shows to sold-out crowds.

Annie believed in hard work, honesty, and generosity. And she always managed to find something to laugh about, even in her darkest times.

Annie Oakley wasn't born in the West. But to many people, she will always be a part of it. Annie died in 1926. And she has been missed ever since.

Annie Oakley's Motto

Aim at the high mark.
And you will hit it.

No, not the first time.
Nor the second.
And maybe not the third.

But keep on aiming.
And keep on shooting.

For only practice
will make you perfect.

Finally, you will
hit the bull's-eye of success.